A NOTE TO PARENTS

Reading Aloud with Your Child

Research shows that reading books aloud is the single most valuable support parents can provide in helping children learn to read.

- Be a ham! The more enthusiasm you display, the more your child will enjoy the book.
- Run your finger underneath the words as you read to signal that the print carries the story.
- Leave time for examining the illustrations more closely; encourage your child to find things in the pictures.
- Invite your youngster to join in whenever there's a repeated phrase in the text.
- Link up events in the book with similar events in your child's life.
- If your child asks a question, stop and answer it. The book can be a means to learning more about your child's thoughts.

Listening to Your Child Read Aloud

The support of your attention and praise is absolutely crucial to your child's continuing efforts to learn to read.

- If your child is learning to read and asks for a word, give it immediately so that the meaning of the story is not interrupted. DO NOT ask your child to sound out the word.
- On the other hand, if your child initiates the act of sounding out, don't intervene.
- If your child is reading along and makes what is called a miscue, listen for the sense of the miscue. If the word "road" is substituted for the word "street," for instance, no meaning is lost. Don't stop the reading for a correction.
- If the miscue makes no sense (for example, "horse" for "house"), ask your child to reread the sentence because you're not sure you understand what's just been read.
- Above all else, enjoy your child's growing command of print and make sure you give lots of praise. *You are your child's first teacher—and the most important one. Praise from you is critical for further risk-taking and learning.*

—Priscilla Lynch
Ph.D., New York University
Educational Consultant

For Danielle and Matthew
—G.H.
To Kelsey
—D.C.

Text copyright © 1995 by Gail Herman.
Illustrations copyright © 1995 by Doug Cushman.
All rights reserved. Published by Scholastic Inc.
HELLO READER!, CARTWHEEL BOOKS, and the CARTWHEEL BOOKS logo
are registered trademarks of Scholastic Inc.

Library of Congress Cataloging-in-Publication Data

Herman, Gail, 1959-
    Teddy bear for sale / by Gail Herman ; illustrated by Doug Cushman.
        p.   cm. — (Hello reader!   Level 1)
    "Cartwheel Books."
    Summary: A teddy bear whom no one wants to buy leaves his shelf in the toy store and sets out for adventure.
        ISBN 0-590-25943-1
        [1. Teddy bears—Fiction.]   I. Cushman, Doug, ill.   II. Title.   III. Series.
PZ7.H4315Te   1995
[E]—dc20   95-10283
                                                                        CIP
                                                                        AC

12 11 10 9 8 7 6 5 4 3 2 1   5 6 7 8 9/9 0 1/0

                    Printed in the U.S.A.   23

First Scholastic printing, December 1995

Teddy Bear for Sale

by Gail Herman
Illustrated by Doug Cushman

Hello Reader! — Level 1

SCHOLASTIC INC.
Cartwheel ·B·O·O·K·S· ®
New York   Toronto   London   Auckland   Sydney

Who will buy
this teddy bear?

Not this girl.
She wants a big red ball.

Not this boy.
He wants a bat.

This girl wants a paint set.

This boy wants a truck.

"Nobody wants me,"
the teddy bear says.
"So I will run away!"

Down the bear jumps!

He jumps into a car.
Off he goes.

The bear drives to a boat

and the boat sets sail.

The bear sails to a train.

The train chugs away.

He stops by a skate

and the skate rolls along.

Then he rolls to a slide.

Down the bear goes!

Down, down, down …

then up, up, up!

Over the skate,
the train, the boat,

and the car.

Over the girls
and over the boys.

Plop!
He lands back on the counter.

"Wow!" says a boy.
"What a great bear!"

Who will buy this teddy bear?

"I will!"
says the boy...

and he takes the bear home.